AS YOU WISH

CAPRICORN COVE SERIES

EVIE MITCHELL

THUNDER THIGHS PUBLISHING

Editing by Nicole Wilson, Evermore Editing
Proofreading by Geeky Girl Author Services
Cover illustration by Laras Petri

ACKNOWLEDGEMENT OF COUNTRY

I acknowledge the Traditional Custodians of the lands on which I write, the Ngunnawal people, and pay my respect to elders both past and present.

I acknowledge the continued and deep spiritual relationship of the Australian Aboriginal and Torres Strait Islander peoples' to this land, and their unique cultural and spiritual relationships to the land, waters and seas and their rich contribution to society.

Always was, always will be.

To my husband
Not for any particular reason beyond I like you and
what's in your pants.

AS YOU WISH

Yasmin

I love cosplay. The costumes, the make-up, the ability to become anyone I want. Which is why Halloween is my favorite time of the year.

And this year? I need to be confident, sensual, and have just a little bit of magic on my side if I'm going to catch the eye of my brother's best friend – Caleb Prince.

He might be the deputy sheriff of our little town, but he's the king of my heart... if only he would look my way.

Caleb

I'm what they call a serial monogamist. I'm not happy unless I'm in a relationship.

Only, none of my relationships have lasted longer than a month, and I know why. Those women weren't Yasmin El Khoury, my best friend's sister.

But when Yasmin walks into my Halloween party dressed as Princess Jasmine – all bets are off. Cause I'm ready to rub every lamp between here and Agrabah if I can just get my one wish... Yasmin.

Warning: This book is inspired by masks, cosplay, and handcuffs. So, get thee a partner and a blindfold or two, and settle in — this book is all treat.

1

Yasmin

"You're *sure* this isn't too revealing?" I asked, tugging on my costume's top for the hundredth time.

"Yasmin," Farrah, my best friend, rolled her eyes from her position on my bed. "One, you look amazing. Like seriously. You nailed this cosplay."

I blushed, accepting her praise. I loved cosplay, give me a comic con and some fabric, and I was happier than a pig in mud.

"And two," Farrah continued, ticking off the reasons on her fingers. "You went with movie princess Jasmine, not cartoon Jasmine. You're practically covered from head to toe. The breast line may be a little low, but it is nowhere *near* revealing."

I sucked in a breath, ridiculously aware of my breasts as they rose with my breath.

"Sorry." I shook my head ruefully. "I know I shouldn't be this paranoid, it's just...."

Farrah sat up, reaching to adjust the top hat on her head. I'd designed her steampunk outfit months ago, painstakingly sewing it around my other projects and my own costume. I had to say, she looked deadly – exactly how an assassin should.

Go me.

"It's just?" she prompted, a small smile playing on her lips. "Does it start with Caleb and end with Prince?"

I grabbed a throw pillow, tossing it at her. "Oh, shut up!"

As was our yearly tradition, we were attending Caleb Prince's party. The man somehow reduced me from being a worldly woman of twenty-six to a bumbling fourteen-year-old, desperate to impress my twin brother's best friend.

If I'd been asked to describe Caleb in one word, I'd use exceptional. I'd always thought he looked a little like Henry Cavill with his stunning blue eyes, tall and solid build and delicious biceps I wanted to lick. But while he might be gorgeous physically, Caleb also happened to be the posture child for 'nice guy'.

When my parents had moved me and my brother to Capricorn Cove we'd been thirteen. I'd fallen into a fast friendship with Farrah, but Malik, my twin, had struggled. Enter Caleb. It'd taken one basketball session for Malik and him to become fast friends, and even now, years later, they were inseparable.

When Malik decided to become a police officer, Caleb joined him. When Caleb had decided to volunteer at the Big Brother program to mentor kids, Malik had done the same. They played fantasy football, were on the same basketball team, and volunteered regularly. They were closer than brothers.

And yep, that made me the sad sack who was in love with my brother's best friend. Was I a cliché? Totally. But I'd held a flame that burned bright for our deputy since the tender age of fourteen.

Seriously, Yasmin. If this doesn't happen tonight, then you need to move the hell on.

No matter how many times I told myself this, I just kept coming back to Caleb.

"Yazzy, it's okay." Farrah gracefully pushed to a stand, the coat tail of her leather jacket falling to the floor behind her. "He's gonna take one look at you and swallow his tongue. He's single. You're single. It's finally time."

I breathed deep, sucking in a long breath and holding it for a beat before slowly letting the air out.

Farrah rolled her eyes, coming to stand beside me. Her hands settled on my hips, and she gently turned me until I faced the mirror.

"You're gorgeous," she said, grinning at my reflection. "You're a badass seamstress, you run your own bridal empire—"

"It's one store," I protested, my lips tugging into a smile.

"Empire!" Farrah declared, ignoring me. "You're intelligent, kind, gracious, and have great tits."

We both looked down at my bountiful handfuls.

"It's true. My breasts are impressive," I agreed.

"Exactly. So tonight," she reached for my cloak, handing it to me with a flourish. "You're Jasmine. Sultry princess, sensual wonder woman, blessed by magic." Her lips twisted into an evil little smile. "And the woman Caleb Prince won't be able to keep his hands off."

I sighed, swinging the brown cape around to settle it on my shoulders. Positioned like this, the material fell in long folds covering me from head to ankle. I looked like Jasmine at the marketplace, hiding who I was. The drama would come when I took it off, revealing my true identity.

And my boobs.

I gave myself a final nod in the mirror then turned to face Farrah.

"Okay, I'm ready. Let's do this."

2

Caleb

"Wait, you invited Willodean?" I stared at my sister, a grin stealing across my face. "Teddy, are you interested in this woman?"

My sister squirmed in place, the giant bowl of Halloween candy I'd just handed her shaking with her movement.

"Maybe."

"Nope!" I shook my head, delighted by this turn of events. "There's no 'maybe' about it. You're smitten!"

"Shut up," she muttered. "Who even says smitten these days?"

"People who are looking at someone who is."

She shook her head and turned away, calling over her shoulder as she walked toward my entryway. "And bring the rest of the candy! We nearly ran out last year."

Chuckling, I checked my to-do list, marking off the last item – *put out candy*. With a last glance around the clean kitchen, I lifted the two giant bowls to follow Teddy, arriving just in time for her to answer the first knock from trick-or-treaters.

"And what have we here?" my sister asked, looking at the cute assortment of costumed toddlers'. "Oh! Who are you?"

"Elsa!" Yelled one of the girls.

"And a gorgeous one at that," Teddy agreed, dumping a massive handful of candy into her little bucket.

And that's why we nearly ran out of candy last year.

"And you are?"

"Toothless," the boy replied, flicking his dragon tail.

"Very scary!"

When their candy demands were met, Teddy headed back inside just as I glanced up, finding the woman of my dreams walking up my drive.

Yasmin.

With over a decade of practice, I pulled my

gaze from Yasmin's hooded figure to take in the others walking beside her – Farrah dressed in some kind of steampunk get-up and Malik dressed as the Splinter to my Raphael.

Teenage Mutant Ninja Turtles for the win!

"Hey dude, great costume." I fist-bumped Malik, nodding in approval and using it as an excuse to look at Yasmin.

"Let me guess, you made it, Yazzy?"

She tilted her head up, her face peeking at me from beneath her hood. "Yeah."

"Good job." I leaned over to run my fingers through Malik's rough fur. "Ooh! It's silky. This is next level."

Malik wrapped an arm around Yasmin's shoulders, pulling her into his side. "Yazzy's the best. I keep telling her to ditch the bridal gowns and go into costume design full-time. She'd make a mint in Hollywood."

My gut clenched, my fists involuntarily clenching.

Over my fucking dead body.

My brain snapped back.

Not your woman, remember?

Malik let her go, looking around me toward the kitchen.

"Do I smell ribs?"

"Yeah, out back. They're just about ready."

He hurried through the house, heading to the backyard, leaving me with Farrah and Yasmin.

"Is Teddy around?" Farrah asked, starting to shuffle down the hall. "Actually, I'll go find her."

She shot a glance at Yasmin, wiggling her eyebrows meaningfully before following Malik and disappearing down the hall.

Yasmin loitered, shuffling from foot to foot, her cloak covering her body.

"You... want to hang your coat up?" I asked finally, needing to break this awkward silence. "It's a surprisingly warm night, and we've got the fire pit going."

"Sure." Yasmin lifted her hands, fiddling with the strings at her throat which held the cloak together.

I reached out to take it, freezing as the fabric slid from her shoulders, revealing her to me. My mouth fell open, my heart stuttered in my chest as my cock hardened.

Holy Moses.

Princess Jasmine stood before me, wearing Yasmin's take on the sultry red outfit from *that* Jafar scene. In a nod to the autumn night, the costume had long sleeves and covered nearly all of her body. But the *way* it covered her? Rawr!

Boobs.

Smile.
Hair.
Curves.
Brain malfunction.

3

Yasmin

I saw Caleb's gaze drop to my breasts and I couldn't help but be both slightly embarrassed and incredibly pleased.

Go with it, Yasmin. Tonight is your chance.

Channelling my inner Princess Jasmine, I tried to roll my hips as I moved closer to Caleb, handing him my cloak.

"I can't believe you're wearing tights," I teased as he took the cloak, his gaze finally meeting mine.

He laughed, smiling as he carefully folded the cloak over his arm. "I'll have you know that tights are in this Halloween."

I took in his outfit, trying not to pay attention to his very pronounced bulge. "Are you gonna bust out some of those ninja moves later?"

"Are you?"

We'd all attended the same dojo, training in various mixed martial arts. The boys had continued, slowly advancing until they both received black belts. Meanwhile, I'd been happy to drop it and retreat back to my preferred form of exercise – swimming. In the fight or flight arena, I was firmly a run-away-as-quickly-as-you-could kind of person.

Caleb cleared his throat, a slight blush touching his cheeks. "You look gorgeous, Yasmin." He coughed, rushing to add, "Not that you don't all the time. It's just... tonight...."

The front door opened, interrupting his verbal flood.

"Yazzy!" Teddy laughed, looking me up and down. "Great costume. You look amazing."

"Thanks." I tilted my head, raising an eyebrow. "An egg?"

Teddy spread her arms out, giving a little shimmer. "Cause I'm egg-cellent. Get it?"

Caleb wrapped an arm around my shoulders, pulling me into his side. "More like she's trying to *poach* the local chicken farmer."

"Willow?" I asked, laughing at Teddy's immediate blush. "Good taste, Ms. Prince. She came in a while ago to get a bridesmaid dress

when her sister was getting married. I was surprised to hear she bought a chicken farm,
though. Seemed more like a corporate type."

Teddy opened her mouth to answer, but the
doorbell rang before she could.

"Looks like the kids are calling me." She
turned, picking up a giant bowl of treats.

With gentle pressure, Caleb steered me
through the house and out to the kitchen.

His arm around me felt casual, friendly. Like
he did this all the time, and he did – to other
people. Caleb was a toucher. He liked to shake
hands and give hugs. He liked to bump fists and
throw arms around people.

And I liked to be held by him, but it happened so rarely that I'd become accustomed to
not expecting it. Or to expect only the briefest
of touches or hugs.

Tonight though? He kept his arm around
me as he stopped us in the kitchen.

"Drink?" he asked, looking down at me.

"Sure."

He dropped his arm, and I felt strangely
bereft without it.

"Soda, beer, or I have some wine." He held
up a bottle of chilled white. "Though I'm not
sure I can recommend it based on the fact it was
a housewarming gift from the guys at the
station."

I chuckled, knowing exactly the kind of pranks my brother and his colleagues pulled on each other. I may have even been roped in once or twice.

"A beer would be great, thanks."

He pulled out a bottle, popped the top and handed it over.

I lifted it, reading the label. "Capricorn Cove Red Dog MicroBrewery? Wait, when did we get a brewery?"

Caleb chuckled, popping the cap on his own beer. "Last month. Though they haven't officially opened yet."

"Then how'd you manage to get these?" I asked, lifting the bottle.

"Connections. It's my cousin's joint."

I lifted the bottle to my lips, taking a swig.

"Wow." I blinked, savouring the fruity notes in the beer. "This is incredible."

Caleb grinned. "Yeah? I'll pass on your approval."

"You do that." I took another pull. "I'm definitely going to have to go out for a tasting."

Caleb cleared his throat, pulling my gaze to him. His eyes darkened, his mouth tightening into a determined line.

"About that." He shifted closer, crowding me into the counter. "Maybe you and I could—"

"Holy shit!" Malik boomed from the entry of

the kitchen, interrupting Caleb. "Dude, these ribs and that beer?" He kissed his fingers. "Per-fucking-fection."

Caleb sighed, his lips twisting into a wry smile. "Thanks, man." He stepped back, giving me some space.

Wait, my heart called. *What were you going to say? WHAT WERE YOU GOING TO SAY????*

I tried to silence my thumping heart. With a small cough, I shifted, rubbing the palm of one hand over the fabric of my harem pants.

Farrah, a plate in each hand, followed my brother.

"Here." She handed me a heaped plate of food. "I saved you some from the bottomless pit over there."

Malik pressed a hand to his chest, a half-eaten rib clutched in his fist. "Moi?"

"Of course you." Farrah rolled her eyes. "You're the one who ate all the chocolate frogs last year and then had the audacity to complain about a stomachache for three days."

Farrah and Malik lived in a share house, along with their roommate, He-Of-The-Terri-ble-Hygiene. The stories they told made me immensely grateful for my little studio apart-ment. I'd repeatedly offered to go in with them, but we'd tried it a few years ago, and they'd both complained about my early morning sewing habit. I'd found living alone to be better.

For years I'd held out a secret hope that they'd fall in love, get married, and have a parcel of babies for me to spoil, thus cementing Farrah as both my best friend and making her my actual sister. Alas, I should have known better—they were far too similar for that nonsense and acted more like brother and sister.

Once, in a fit of matchmaking, I'd dropped some hints to Farrah, hoping to push her in the right direction. She'd physically gagged, and I'd never brought up the subject again.

"Oh, am I interrupting?"

I turned, seeing Hannah Sharp hovering in the entry. She wore a pumpkin pinned to her head and a shirt covered in numbers.

"No, come on in, Hannah. Beer?" Malik asked, moving to the fridge.

"Oh, um, yes. Please. Thank you."

She placed a dish on the counter, pushing it across to Caleb. "I brought those cookies you guys like. I hope that's okay."

"Fuck yes!" Malik called, his head popping up from behind the fridge door. "Those chocolate fudge ones?"

She nodded, a little blush flushing her cheeks.

"Ace." He grinned, nodding at her costume. "Nice. Pumpkin pie, right?"

She nodded again, her blush deepening.

"Thanks, Hannah." Caleb lifted the plate, unwrapping the tea towel that covered the cookies. "I'll just pop them out on the table."

"I can do that. Are the kids outside?" She reached for the plate, lifting it up, and turned to leave the kitchen, seemingly in a rush to avoid further conversations.

"Yeah."

With a nod, she left, leaving behind a faint pumpkin-spice scent and Malik holding her beer.

"I didn't realise you knew Hannah," I said to my brother with a frown. "And well enough for her to know your favourite cookie type."

Malik shrugged, popping the cap on Hannah's beer. "Girl brings baked goods to the station every week. Has ever since Tristan took over from her dad about," he glanced at Caleb for confirmation. "What? Three, four years?"

"Something like that," Caleb agreed. "She's also the regional coordinator for Big Brothers Big Sisters."

I blinked, exchanging a wide-eyed look with Farrah.

"Really?"

"Yeah, she's a cool chick," Malik replied with a shrug.

"Hannah? As in Hannah Sharp?" Farrah asked, trying to clarify. "As in Hannah, who is well known to have been the biggest bully in our high school."

Malik shook his head. "That's not how I remember it, but you're older than me and probably getting a touch senile in your old age."

"Dude, I'm three months older than you." Farrah flipped him the bird. "But seriously, don't you remember when she terrorised the school during that 'Save the Earth' fundraiser?"

"Militant," I agreed with a nod. "She actually yelled at me for not meeting my target."

"Look." Malik shook his head. "One, high school was over a decade ago. People change. Who knows, maybe she had a reason to be how she was back then. Did you ask?"

I slowly shook my head

"Also," he continued. "Being passionate and being a bully are two different things."

He shuffled to the doorway, pausing to pick up his half-eaten plate on the way out. "To be honest, I'm kinda disappointed that the women in my life are being this shallow. Maybe pull your heads out and get to know her instead of casting judgments on a woman based on the shit she did in high school. I'm not the same person I was back then, and I know damn sure neither of you are either."

With that parting shot, Malik left the room.

"Ouch," Farrah rubbed at her chest, grimacing. "Boy knows how to hit you right where it hurts."

"Bonfires out back," Caleb said, tilting his beer bottle toward the door. "Some of the families have already arrived. We could go out, and you could hang with her."

I exchanged a glance with Farrah, years of friendship allowing us to communicate silently.

We're asses.

Yep.

Let's go be nice.

Agreed. Who knows, maybe we'll get a new friend out of tonight?

Yes, definitely. Also, Caleb thinks you're cute. He keeps looking at your breasts.

I rolled my eyes at her eyebrow wiggle.

Shut up.

But as we walked outside, I couldn't help but notice that Caleb did indeed seem to be glancing down at my breasts.

Just as I wished.

4

Yasmin

The party was in full swing with couples dancing, people mingling, and kids racing around, high on sugar and excitement.

I knew how they felt. My body had turned into a little pool of warm, tingling anticipation. Every time Caleb looked at me, I could see the heat in his eyes and feel a spark in the air. An awareness that had danced at the periphery of our interactions for years. But tonight?

It feels magical.

It might have been the twinkling fairy lights strung around the yard, the wonder and mysticism that attached itself to this time of year, or perhaps it was just the night itself that shrouded us in possibilities. But this Halloween, I wanted nothing more than to discover my inner witch and make Caleb burn.

In only the best way possible, of course.

We'd been rotating around each other all evening, Caleb busy with his guests while I chatted, catching up with friends.

But every few minutes, I'd catch a glance of his ridiculous mask and green-painted face and glance his way, our eyes meeting. It was as if something had snapped into place when I'd walked through his door, like the world aligned and granted us permission to have our one wish.

Or perhaps it's all wishful thinking on my part.

With his major hosting duties over, Caleb walked my way, all loose hips, and easy smiles. I shifted, making space beside me for him, the action unconscious and so instinctual that I didn't even process the movement.

He stepped into the space, filling it, his arm brushing mine.

"Hey," I said with a small smile. "Great party."

"Thanks." He lifted his beer, taking a sip as he considered me over the bottle. "And if I haven't said it already, you look great, Yasmin. Gorgeous."

His voice sounded husky, its rough edge sending a pleasant shiver down my spine.

Come on, Yasmin, let's bring on a few more magical sparks.

I shifted closer to him, close enough to feel the warmth of his body.

"Thanks." I reached over to tap his paper shell, dimly aware that the rest of our circle were laughing at a joke someone had made. "This is cute."

He grinned. "If I'd have asked, would you have created me something elaborate?"

"Caleb, I'd have turned you into an actual turtle."

We both chuckled, our gaze locked on each other. Awareness flared between us, desire and comfortable familiarity mixing together to create something new and unfamiliar.

I found I liked the anticipatory fluttering in my stomach.

Malik pushed himself between us, wrapping an arm around my shoulders, my doofus brother completely incapable of picking up on the vibe between Caleb and me.

With a sigh, I broke off eye contact with Caleb, looking up at my twin with a shake of my head and an eye roll.

"What?" he asked, glancing around. "Am I interrupting something?"

"Don't worry about it." I bumped my hip against him. "You're too immature to understand."

He laughed, giving me a little squeeze. "Probably true."

"Definitely true," Caleb interrupted from Malik's side. "You're like a man-child. Constantly hangry, desperate for attention, always wants a new toy."

"Hey!" Malik lifted the arm he'd wrapped around me, pressing it to his chest. "I can't help being distracted by new shiny things."

"If that isn't his dating life summed up in a sentence, I don't know what is," Farrah muttered.

I laughed, holding up a hand for a high-five.

Malik, pretending to be wounded by her words, looked around the fire, searching for support.

"Hannah! Back me up, tell these nincompoops that I'm mature."

She looked at him wide-eyed for a moment as if surprised to be included in the conversation. Then a small grin played at her lips, one sculptured eyebrow arching.

"In age or emotional maturity? Because I'm yet to see evidence of the last."

We laughed, Malik, faking outrage as Caleb raised his beer in Hannah's direction.

"Great burn, Hannah!"

Teddy walked up, hand-in-hand with Willodean. I couldn't help but giggle at their costumes. Willow was dressed as a sexy chicken, Teddy as her egg-cellent self. They were an adorable pair.

"Alright." Teddy reached into her egg costume, pulling out sheets of paper. "Who's up for the annual scavenger hunt?"

With a laugh, all hands shot up.

The annual scavenger hunt had been going on since we were kids. We took turns organising who ran it each year so we could all participate. This year it was Teddy's turn, and I suspected she didn't mind as it would give her more quality time with Willow. "Teams?"

Malik dropped me faster than a hot potato, pointing at Hannah. "Me and Hannah, we got this."

Hannah's eyes were wide once again, her face frozen in surprise. "Me?"

"Wait, don't tell me Farrah claimed you already?"

"N-no?"

"Good." He looked at Farrah, sticking his tongue out at her. "Hannah's a certified genius. Honestly, we got this."

"Good luck, 'cause I've got...." She looked

around the group, settling on a guy standing quietly near us. "Spiderman."

The guy, dressed in full Spiderman costume – including face mask – jolted. "What?"

"You heard me." She reached for the sheet Teddy held out, pulling a pencil from one of her many pockets. "I need a partner."

"Guess that means you're with me." Caleb's words brushed the shell of my ear, the heat of him warming my back. Pleasant goosebumps rose on my skin, those sparks flaring.

I've always been with you.

I turned, looking up at him with a small grin. "I guess that does."

He accepted the offered paper from his sister, nodding at the assembled couples. "Chances of winning?"

I seized up our competition. "Farrah will take it out again. Malik and Hannah don't have a hope in hell."

He laughed, his hand settling on my hip and drawing me into him as he handed me the paper. "Didn't we give Farrah a handicap last year?"

I laughed. "Yeah... we just 'forgot' to tell her we'd started." I made air quotes with my fingers.

"And she still won." He chuckled. "But this year, that trophy is ours!"

The trophy in question was nothing more

than a collection of junk glued together and spray-painted gold. Each year, another item was added by the victor, and the reigning champion got to hang onto the monstrosity until the next Halloween.

Only Farrah ever displayed it prominently, and considering she'd been the champion for the last five years, I guess that meant it was a part of her décor.

"Alright, you know the rules, but because this is Hannah and Spiderman's first time, let me go over them again." Teddy held up a hand. "One, you have an hour to find everything on that list and get back here. Two, the more creative the interpretation, the better the points. Three, photos need to be texted to the number at the bottom of the list. Four, you are encouraged to sabotage, trick, and wrestle other teams. Bribes to the judges are also encouraged. The only rule is don't do anything that could get you arrested – Farrah, I'm looking at you."

She poked her tongue out at Teddy. "It was one time!"

Teddy grinned. "And as always, the judges' decision is final. Alright, on your marks, get set... go!"

I unfolded the paper, holding it up to the light, Caleb leaning over my shoulder to read.

"Oh, God." Giggles bubbled up my throat, spilling out. "It's egg-themed!"

5

Caleb

My sister was completely scrambled. I read through the list, wondering where on earth we'd find even half the shit she'd dreamed up.

"Okay, let's see," Yasmin tapped her finger against the first clue. "The chicken crossing the road is getting married."

I glanced at Yasmin in confusion. "A chicken in a wedding dress?"

"A hens' party," she said, grinning. "They want a picture of a hens party."

"Oh, for fucks... right. Of course, it is." I looked back at the list. "A rooster, something scrambled, something truly egg-cellent, something to represent fowl play, something I could mis-lay." I shook my head. "Honestly, these are getting worse."

"Keep reading," Yasmin told me with a giggle.

"Something to put all your eggs in, something to crack me up, a very-eggy celebrity."

"Oh!" Yasmin snapped her fingers, looking around. "There! Let's get a picture with Doctor Strange."

I glanced at the guy, frowning. "What's that got to do with this?"

"Benedict Cumberbatch played Doctor Strange!" Yasmin bounced on her toes, grinning. "Get it? Eggs Benedict?"

I barked out a laugh, capturing her hand and pulling her toward the guy. "Good spot."

I snapped a picture of her and the guy, trying not to let my annoyance show when he put an arm around her.

"Alright, next?" I asked, shooting the photo text off to Teddy.

"The chicken crossing the road might be hard. Where do we find a hen's party on Halloween?"

I rubbed my chin. "Let's come back to that. How about a rooster?"

"You mean a cock?"

I froze when Yasmin's gaze dropped to my crotch, my body immediately responding.

"I... I doubt Teddy meant that."

Yasmin flushed, glancing away but not before I saw a hint of heat in her gaze.

"Wait." Inspiration struck. "I might have a two-in-one solution."

I caught her hand, entwining our fingers as I led her through the party and out to the street. In the distance, I saw Farrah and Spiderman heading down the road toward the beach, Farrah practically dragging him along behind her.

Oh, game on.

Two houses down sat Mrs. Anderson's place. Mrs. Anderson also happened to be the owner of a large lawn ornament collection which she cycled through regularly.

I led Yasmin to the door, knocking.

"You know," Mrs. Anderson grinned, an arm cradling a bowl of candy. "I do think you're a little old for trick or treating, Caleb. No matter how well dressed you and your lady friend are."

I laughed, wrapping an arm around Yazzy and pulling her into my side. "Mrs. Anderson, this is Yasmin, Yasmin, Mrs. Anderson."

"Hi," Yasmin gave her a little wave.

"Lovely to meet you, dear." She gave me a meaningful look.

"Mrs. Anderson, do you happen to still have those chickens you used for your Easter display? We're in a scavenger hunt, and I wanted to borrow one."

"Oh," she paused, thinking. "Yes, I do believe I might have one or two out in the garden shed." She flapped a hand at us. "If you can find it, you can have it. I'm going with a bunny theme this year."

With permission secured we raided her shed, finding a small rooster and a pastel pink hen.

"Yes!" Yazzy held the chicken up in triumph. "We can knock off a few with this."

In quick succession, we managed to collect photos of a chicken crossing the road, an egg key-chain (something that could be mis-laid), a woman dressed as a Bachelorette contestant (hens party), a small basket (to put all your eggs in), and a soccer ball (fowl play). The last one was a stretch but time was ticking and beggars couldn't be choosers.

"That just leaves something scrambled and something truly egg-cellent," Yasmin read, glancing up at me with a frown. "What's truly egg-cellent?"

My gaze dropped unintentionally to the swell of her magnificent tits.

She caught my look, laughing. "They are, but get your head in the game, Mr. Prince. We need to win this."

With regret, I pulled my gaze away, looking around. I spied a young girl dressed as a scrambled Rubik's cube.

"Yes!" I snagged Yasmin's hand and pulled her in the kid's direction. We snapped a picture, my phone beeping to let me know we only had five minutes left.

"We're gonna have to run!"

We hot-footed it back to my house, both of us laughing and a little breathless.

"Wait!" Yasmin, skidded to a halt, looking up at me, her eyes frantic. "We need something truly egg-cellent!"

I ran a hand through my hair, looking around.

"I've got it!" Yazzy shoved open my front door, dashing for my lounge. "Do you still have that DVD of Bill and Ted's Excellent Adventure that Malik gave you?"

"Yes!" We both dove for my entertainment unit, pulling out drawers and rifling through them.

"Hurry!" Yasmin yelled, her fingers flicking through my extensive collection.

"Got it!" I held the DVD up, scooping the rooster under one arm and catching her hand with my other. "Let's go."

Laughing, running, and stumbling, we

made it to the backyard, both of us groaning as we realised we were the last team.

With a growing sense of resignation, we handed over our items, Teddy and Willow accepting them and then shooing us off to confer.

"Who made it back first?" I asked Malik as he handed me a beer.

"Hannah and I." He grinned proudly. "Girl is a motherfucking scavenger genius."

She blushed beside Malik, looking pleased but embarrassed.

"Alright, you guys," Teddy called our attention back to her. "And the winner is..."

6

Caleb

I'd worked with a lotta kids over the years. Kids who came from broken homes, kids who'd learned to put up armour, kids with socialisation difficulties.

Hannah Sharp ticked all those boxes. The woman had grown up in a divorced household, ferried between a father who was more interested in being Sheriff than dad, and a mother who'd remarried or shared up with men more times than I had fingers and toes – including once to two guys who'd lived in a commune.

It was why it didn't surprise me that she'd never participated in a scavenger hunt, let alone played truth or dare.

"No way in hell you've never played this

game!" Yasmin declared from beside me, pointing a finger at Hannah. "Seriously, this is like *the game* we played in high school."

The party had wound down, the families heading home to tuck babies into bed while the couples snuck off to find quiet places – including my sister and her new love interest. I'd be teasing her about *that* later.

Which left the singles – Malik, Hannah, Wolf – still dressed as Spiderman, Farrah, Yasmin, and me – sitting around the fire roasting marshmallows and playing stupid games.

"I didn't attend high school parties," Hannah said with a shrug. Beside her, the Scavenger trophy glinted in the firelight, the biggest, ugliest piece of crap trophy you'd ever seen.

I grinned, catching Farrah sending it a sad look.

"Well, consider this a trip down memory lane," Malik told Hannah, slapping a hand on his knee. "And I shall graciously go first." He looked at me.

"Truth or dare, Caleb?"

I lifted my beer bottle, shooting him a grin. "Truth." I tipped it, taking a swig while he pursed his lips, considering me.

"Is it true that you got to shake Wayne Gretzky's hand, or was that bull shit?"

I chuckled as Farrah and Yasmin groaned,

rolling their eyes. "It's true, you motherfucker, and you know it. Your turn."

Hannah watched, wide-eyed as we went around the circle, each of us daring the other.

"Your turn," Yasmin told her with a grin. "Truth or dare, Hannah?"

She pursed her lips. "Dare."

"Ooohhh!" Malik pretended to be shocked. "She's got lady balls!"

"Alright, I dare you..." Yasmin glanced around, finally narrowing her eyes on her brother, who was helping himself to the final three cookies. "I dare you to take those cookies from Malik and give them to me."

All heads twisted to stare at Malik, laughter bubbling around the group as he stared at his sister, hand frozen halfway to his mouth.

"Excuse me?" he asked, outraged. "What the fuck, Yaz?"

She giggled, nodding at Hannah. "Go on, Hannah! Quick! Before he eats them."

Hannah nodded, holding out a hand to Malik. "I'll take those, please, and thank you."

"What? No!"

Hannah frowned at him, "It's my dare. Are you not going to help me with my dare?"

"Nope." He moved to stuff the cookies in his mouth, but Hannah was faster. Her hand shot out, gripping and twisting his wrist, and snatching the falling cookies from the air.

"What the fuck!?" Malik howled, cradling his wrist. "Where'd you learn that?"

"Dojo," Hannah replied, cradling the cookies in a napkin. She began to walk toward a cackling Yasmin, who had tears running down her cheeks. "Here you go... Yazzy."

Yasmin held out her hand, about to take the cookies when Malik scooped up Hannah, throwing her over his shoulder and heading off into the dark shadows of the yard.

"Don't come looking for us!" Malik yelled over his shoulder. "We're negotiating cookies!"

Around the fire, we fell into fits of laughter.

"Alright, your turn," Yasmin said, wiping tears from her cheeks, her grin huge as she looked at Farrah. "Who's next?"

Farrah glanced around, her gaze narrowing on a guy in Spiderman gear. Wolf Rodriguez was back in town after a world tour with his band. He may be a rock star and one of my oldest friends, yet, for some reason, he sat around my fire acting like he didn't want anyone to know who he was.

I knew there was a story there, but I didn't push him. The thing about Wolf was he'd tell me in his own time.

"Truth or Dare, Spidey?" Farrah asked, her

lips pursing, one eyebrow arched in his direction.

"Truth," he said, the mask hiding any expression.

She hesitated for a moment, and I knew she was about to blow his cover. I shifted a warning on the tip of my tongue, my body tensing.

"Who's better, Captain America or Iron Man?" she finally asked.

Wolf chuckled, leaning forward. "Captain America. Integrity, super speed. And he got his girl in the end."

Farrah's lips twitched, one side pulling up into a half-smile. "Okay, your turn."

Wolf considered the group through his mask.

"CALEB, TRUTH OR DARE?"

"Go on then, dare." I grinned, shooting Jazzy a wink.

"I dare you to spend seven minutes in heaven with Princess Jasmine over there."

Everyone froze, the fire crackling ominously.

I coughed, clearing my throat. "Sorry, what?"

He shrugged. "Seven minutes in heaven. That's normally what people got dared to do back in the day, right?"

I threw a look at Yasmin, who was staring at me.

"Look, that's really a dare for both of us, and I don't want to make Yasmin—"

"Oh, come on." She handed her beer to Farrah, pushing up from her seat. "Seven minutes. I'll yell when you can start the timer."

I made to take my shell off but she stopped me.

"No, leave it on."

Um. What??

She took my hand with a wink, pulling me up and leading me around the side of my house to a dark shadowed area.

"Yasmin." I finally got a hold of myself, halting her with a gentle tug on her hand. "You don't have to do this."

In the light of the moon, she looked up at me, her eyes wide, her teeth glinting a little as they bit her lower lip.

"But what if I want to?"

Wait. Did she just say...? Oh, fuck yes!

7

Yasmin

My heart pounded loudly in my ears, and my palms were damp. Pterodactyls flapped frantically in my stomach, doubts rampaging through my mind.

Oh God, Yasmin, what have you done? Shit shit shit shit shit!

I opened my mouth to say... something. Anything. Any-goddamned-thing. But Caleb beat me to it.

"When you say you want this." He shifted, his hands coming to frame my waist, crowding me until my back met the cool brick of his house. "What *exactly* do you mean?"

I swallowed, forcing myself to lift my head to meet his gaze.

I opened my mouth, the words I wanted to say sticking in my throat.

I want you to kiss me.

Caleb narrowed his gaze on me, his expression shifting.

"Cause I want you and me to become an us. I want to kiss you, Yasmin. I want to lick your pussy. I want to taste your breasts. I want to know if you're spicy or sweet. Way I see it, we got two options here, Jazzy. First, I step back, and we put all this in a box that we'll never discuss again."

"And the second?" I asked, my voice barely a whisper.

"Second is I kiss you, and we find out that seven minutes is never gonna be long enough." He leaned forward, his lips hovering a mere inch away from mine. "Consent is sexy, babe. So, what's it gonna be?"

My answer was to close the gap between us.

My lips met his, and for the briefest moment, it remained a simple, chaste kiss. Just a meeting of pursed lips and sweet desire.

Then it turned carnal.

I may have started the kiss, but Caleb quickly took over. He anchored me, one hand at my hip, the other fisting my braid. With gentle pressure, he tilted my head back a fraction, giving him better access to my lips, all the while pressing hot and hungry kisses to my mouth.

"Open," he ordered, his tone guttural and utterly demanding.

I did, moaning as his tongue slipped in, his body pressing closer to mine, his erection hard against my stomach.

Oh, Lord have mercy.

I was so going to hell for this.

Caleb kissed me as if he'd never stop. He devoured my mouth, his tongue dancing with mine. He overpowered and overwhelmed me, and I loved it, a delicious throbbing ache taking root in my body.

More.

As if hearing my plea, his hands moved, coming up to frame my breasts, cupping them, his thumbs running over the material separating his skin from mine.

"This fucking costume," he whispered against my lips, his breathing heavy. "I wanna tear it off you and fuck you right here. I wanna hear you beg for me to feed you my cock. Do you have any idea how fucking long I've wanted you? How many times I've fisted myself to thoughts of you?"

I had no words of comfort to offer him, just a body that throbbed with the need he'd awoken in it.

I caught one of his hands, sliding it down my body to the waistband of my pants.

"Touch me."

With a muttered curse, his hand slid down my stomach, slipping between the material to cup my pussy.

"Fuck, Yasmin."

I could feel how wet I was, my underwear soaked, need slicking my thighs. His rough fingers pressed my underwear to the side, baring me to his touch.

"Shh," he whispered against my lips as he found my clit. "Quiet, or someone might hear."

I leaned forward, my teeth digging into his chest as he began to circle my clit, his teasing finger hitting me just right.

How did he know?

A moment later, I didn't care as my body shuddered, his fingers grazing the spot where I desperately ached to be touched.

"Again?" he whispered against my ear.

I nodded, incapable of speaking.

With a hungry chuckle, he circled, soft at first, grazing that little bud, hitting the spot on the left that felt so fucking good to me. Once, twice, I lost count, desire winding me up, spiralling tighter and tighter.

I wanted to scream at him. To demand he make me come. I was a moment away from it when he sank his teeth into my earlobe, gently tugging.

A wet heat flooded my panties, my body bursting into a million pieces as I came, clenching and gasping, shaking under his talented hands.

"Good girl," he praised, one hand cradling me, the other still fingering my clit. "Once more, then we'll take you back to the fire."

More than seven minutes had passed, but Gods, I didn't care. He fingered me and kissed me, praised me, and cursed me. Every moment was too much and not enough.

I had dreamt of Caleb for so long that this felt like a dream.

This was too easy. Too quick. Too fast. Too—

I shattered for the second time, his mouth covering mine to swallow my scream. He caught me, supporting my shaking, vulnerable body as I came.

"That's it, Yazzy. Milk it, babe."

A sob caught in my throat. My emotions on high alert following the amazing orgasms.

This is Caleb. Caleb is touching you. Caleb just made you come.

I clung to him, dimly aware of his lips against my heated skin, nuzzling into me as he straightened my clothes, setting me back to right.

"Yazzy?"

I finally snapped back, twisting slightly in his arms to meet his gaze.

"You okay, baby?" He asked, brushing stray strands of hair from my face.

"Oh, um... yeah. I think so." I stammered, a flush heating my cheeks. "Are you? I mean... do you need... you know?"

He grinned; it was slightly crooked but oh so attractive. My heart skipped, my body beginning to throb once more.

"Fuck yeah, I'm good." He shook his head, his expression rueful. "And no. I came like I was back in eighth grade and getting my first glimpse of boob."

I laughed, relieved that the ease that defined our relationship hadn't diminished just because we'd made third base.

Gods, third base? Really, Yasmin? Are you back in high school?

I leaned into Caleb, enjoying the feel of him against me. "You know that's kind of hot, right? That you're so into me you apparently can't help yourself."

He hesitated, then huffed out a laugh. "Truth? I've never been able to control myself around you. The number of times I've jerked off to thoughts of you is incalculable."

I blinked, warmth filling my chest. "Wait. Really?"

"Oh, yeah." He shook his head. "And don't think I don't know that it makes me the biggest fucking douchebag, but I have no chill."

I wasn't sure if it was the two orgasms, but I found I didn't have it in me to care.

"I like that," I admitted, snuggling closer. "I like that you were as into me as I was with you."

"Were?"

I laughed, pressing a kiss to his jaw. "Fine, *am* into you."

"Better." He sighed, nuzzling my cheek. "Fuck, I shoulda made an approach years ago."

I pulled back a little, frowning. "Why didn't you?"

8

Caleb

"Why didn't you?"

Great fucking question.

I opened my mouth to reply, only to be interrupted by Farrah bellowing from across the yard.

"That's seven minutes!"

Yasmin sighed, rolling her eyes. "Come on, we better get back before she comes searching."

I pulled back, wrapping an arm around her and pulling her into my side. "You gonna have a problem with us announcing that we're dating?"

Yasmin tipped her head back, grinning up at me. "Not at all."

"Good." I rubbed my thumb over her face. "I got a little green on you."

She smirked. "Leave it. I like the idea of you marking me."

Annnndddd there's my cock again.

We returned to the fire; her fingers entwined with mine. Farrah sent me a knowing look, a little smile playing on her face.

In the short time we'd been gone, Malik and Hannah had returned, Spiderman had somehow found a guitar, and Farrah had a new packet of marshmallows open beside her.

I pulled Yasmin onto my lap, chancing a glance at Malik. The guy wasn't even paying attention, his focus narrowed in on the marshmallows.

"You gonna share those?" he asked Farrah as she threaded the treats onto her stick.

"If you ask nicely, maybe."

"Please, can I have some?"

She paused, pursed her lips and tilted her head, frowning as if deep in thought.

"No."

We laughed at Malik's expression before Farrah began to pass out loaded sticks.

Yasmin accepted ours, and I noticed that Farrah had only handed us the one stick, but threaded two marshmallows on the end.

Smart lady.

Wolf pulled off his mask, brushing his face

and shaking his hair. The fucker was good-looking, and the millions he now owned couldn't hurt his chances.

"You gonna play something?" Malik asked him, nodding at the guitar.

He shrugged, his fingers absently plucking chords. "Maybe."

"What else haven't you played?" Farrah asked Hannah, holding her stick to the fire.

"I never went to any high school parties, so... everything?"

"We could play spin the bottle?" I suggested pressing a kiss to Yasmin's shoulder.

"Ew, no." Yasmin swatted my arm. "I refuse to play that when a relative is in the circle."

"What about Never Have I Ever?" Wolf asked, his fingers still on the guitar.

"Ooooh! Good one!" Malik reached into the cooler beside his leg, pulling out beer bottles and beginning to pass them around the group.

"How's this work?" Hannah asked, looking from the beer to Wolf.

"Watch," Farrah directed. "Never have I ever been at a professional photo shoot."

Around the circle, Wolf, Malik, and I lifted our beers, taking a sip.

"Wait." Hannah leaned forward, her blonde hair slipping free of her shoulder as she looked around. "You have definitely been pho-tographed," she said, pointing at Wolf. "Which means you guys have as well?"

"They were in a 'Hot Cops' calendar," Yasmin giggled, her body relaxing into mine. "They complained about the saucy geriatrics who sent them love letters for months after."

"Not to mention the baby oil." Malik shuddered.

"So you drink if you've done it?" Hannah clarified, her eyes wide.

"Yep. Your turn."

She pursed her lips, nodding. "Never have I ever kissed a girl."

Around the fire, all the guys, including me and Farrah drank.

"Wait, what?" Yasmin stared at her friend. "You never told me this!"

"No biggie. It was back in sophomore year. Hazel Jeffrey got wasted drunk and cornered me in the hall on the way to the bathroom. She laid one on me." Farrah laughed. "Wasn't bad, but definitely made me realise that I was totally het-erosexual."

It was Malik's turn.

"Never have I ever dated my best friend's sister."

I groaned, raising the bottle to my lips to take a sip. "Poorly done, bro."

Malik laughed. "You gotta let me torture you a little. It's only taken you a fucking lifetime."

"To confirm, you're cool with me and Yazzy?" I clarified the tension I hadn't realised I'd been holding loosening in my shoulders.

"Of course." He nodded at his sister. "I trust Yasmin to know who and what she wants in a partner. And you're my best friend, dude. You're a good guy. I trust you. You make this last I get my best friend for a brother. You fuck this up, I'll beat the shit outta you."

I tightened my arm around Yasmin's middle. "Noted."

With that settled, it was my turn.

"Never have I ever gotten a speeding ticket."

Yasmin groaned, rolling her eyes and lifting her beer. "You're a monster."

I laughed. "You should have known your connections wouldn't have gotten you out of that ticket."

She poked her tongue out at me, and I leaned forward, capturing her mouth and nipping at her lips.

Around the circle it went, the declarations more outrageous as the game progressed.

"Never have I ever ridden an elephant," Hannah said, swaying a little in her chair.

Both Wolf and Farrah drank.

"What!" Hannah shrieked. "When?"

"When I volunteered in Bali for nine months. I helped at an elephant hospital. Part of it included taking the elephants down to the river and giving them a bath. To properly scrub their back and check for parasites, you need to get up on them."

"That's so freaking cool," Hannah mumbled, playing with her label.

"Mine's less cool, it was for a promo." Wolf shrugged. "The upside was the elephant apparently loved my music. The handler said he plays me for her, and she dances in her field. The downside is the elephant was only there because we were doing an awareness campaign to raise money for the sanctuary. They're all ex-circus animals."

"Well, that got morose quickly," Malik said after a moment's silence. "Play us something, you cheap ass. And let me record it so I can sell the video to TMZ and buy a house."

Wolf laughed, repositioning the guitar and beginning to strum. "Any requests?"

"Dark Love?" Hannah asked, naming one of his popular songs.

"How about we steer away from my songs, and I do covers."

"Perfect, Ed Sheeran." I directed, pressing another kiss to Yazzy's shoulder.

She looked at me, her eyes liquid pools of love. "Good choice."

"If it's gonna be our song, gotta make it good."

Wolf began to strum, his soulful voice filling the night.

"Go on, Farrah." He directed with a nod when he reached the part where Beyonce would normally sing.

She laughed, rolling her eyes. "Brace all, I haven't sung in years."

He played the bridge again, nodding at her cue.

She opened her mouth, closed her eyes, and gave in, her husky voice raising goosebumps.

"I forgot how good she is," Yasmin whispered, her body swaying gently as Wolf and Farrah sang.

"Mm."

The song finished, and Wolf immediately shifted into Eminem's Love the Way You Lie.

"I can't do Rihanna!" Farrah laughed, shaking her head before she opened her lips to deliver a pretty fucking convincing effort.

Yasmin cuddled in, her head tucked against my neck, her fingers absently tracing shapes on my arm.

As the night turned into early morning,

Yasmin fell asleep cuddled into me. Under the moon, surrounded by music, I found that I had everything I'd ever wanted in my arms.

Never have I ever been in love.

I lifted my beer to my lips, grinning as I took a sip.

9

Yasmin

"No," the bride gasped, shaking her head. "Oh Lordy, Yasmin! This is...."

I reached for the tissues, experience with emotional brides ensuring I always had a box or two available.

As predicted, she burst into tears, her hands fluttering around her face. "Oh, Gods. I'm sorry!"

"Don't be." I handed her the box. "The greatest joy an artist can get is from someone appreciating their work."

The bride huffed out a wet laugh. "He's gonna love it."

"He's gonna love *you*," I corrected. "The dress is just a nice bonus."

"And the lingerie." She grinned.

"Oh, my yes!"

We both chuckled, tears forgotten.

"Come on." I reached down, collecting her train. "Let's show your family."

My favourite part of being a seamstress was creating a piece that would feature in their most precious memories. Oh sure, ten years from now, they probably wouldn't remember this fitting or the lace detail on the dress, but they'd remember walking down the aisle and seeing their partner's face. They'd remember dancing and cake, love and laughter, friends and family.

They'd remember the emotion. And that, for me, was the most beautiful part of my creations.

I left the bride and her entourage laughing in the bridal suite – a special area I'd specifically created to enhance moments like this – and returned to the main store, checking in on my assistant.

"How'd it go?" Mae asked, placing a selection of little dance dresses on a short rack.

"Bride loved it. They're having some champagne and treats while the bridesmaids try on their dresses."

I looked around the room, clocking two men and a little girl heading up the sidewalk.

My lips lifted, and a little flutter started in my belly.

"Ah, I spot Tattooed Dance Dad at twelve o'clock," Mae laughed, already moving to the entry.

"I don't recognise the guy with him. Is he a new dance dad?"

"No, that's Caleb."

Mae blinked, her big eyes widening as she stared at me. "As in *the* Caleb?"

I laughed, nodding.

Having made it to the store, the little girl shoved open the door, pausing dramatically in the entry.

"Is it here?" she asked, staring directly at Mae.

"She is!" Mae confirmed, laughing as the young girl screeched her excitement, bouncing up and down on her toes, sending her pigtails flying.

Mae had a tendency to refer to clothing as people. She said they spoke to her, letting her know who would wear them best.

"I take it her dress arrived?" the Tattooed Dance Dad asked with a rueful grin.

"It is, and she's beautiful," Mae confirmed. "Right this way."

Our small town seemed to have a plethora of young single dads. All of whom took their daughters to the local dance school. Mae and I had gotten so used to them coming in for costumes or special dress orders that we'd started nicknaming the dads. Tattooed Dance Dad was Mae's favourite.

"Hey, stranger." I greeted Caleb with a quick kiss. "Did we have plans?"

He looked around the store, shaking his head. "Nope. Just thought I'd come and see if you were free for dinner tonight."

"You could have texted."

He grinned, slipping a hand around my back to pull me against him. "But then I wouldn't have been able to do this."

The kiss was long and deliciously unhurried, less of a kiss and more of a savouring.

"Hey." He pressed his forehead against mine.

"Wow," I replied, flushing. "That's a hell of a hello."

I heard Mae bustle back in, heading to the bridal suite.

"This place is big," Caleb commented, drawing back and looking around. "I always forget how big it is."

Last year, when the candle shop next door had closed down, I'd taken a gamble. I'd purchased the store, bumped out our walls, and added a second shop specifically for children. I'd noticed a jump in requests for kids' outfits – particularly dance clothes. The gamble had paid off, with sales well ahead of my projected forecast.

Caleb had been roped in to help with a variety of jobs during the construction phase. And, now that I thought on it, he hadn't ever grumbled.

I opened my mouth to question him when Mae reappeared, giving me the head tilt sign that the bride and her party were ready for measurements.

I sighed, withdrawing from Caleb. "Yes to dinner, but I have to get back to work."

"All good." He grinned, leaning down to kiss me again. "I respect that you're a boss babe, and gotta do what you gotta do. I'll drop by your place tonight around seven." He kissed my nose then stepped back, looking around the store again. "And, just saying." He sent me a wink. "You'd look killer in that dress."

With those parting words, he left, leaving me staring at his back as he headed back toward the police station, his butt looking particularly fine in his uniform.

"Phew." Mae fanned herself as she fell in beside me, watching Caleb's butt. "You guys are so hot together you burn me up."

I laughed, bumping her with my hip. "Is the bride ready?"

She made a face. "Yep." She dropped her voice, leaning in to whisper. "And the mum-zilla isn't happy with the lacing."

I rolled my eyes. "I'll take care of it, thanks."

"I expect details later!"

Laughing, I returned to the bridal party and the mum-zilla from hell.

10

Caleb

"You coming?" Malik asked, slinging his gym bag over his shoulder.

I finished tying my shoe, glancing at the clock on the wall. "Rain check. I got a hot date."

Malik rolled his eyes. "Let me guess, my sister is making you dinner?"

"Nope." I dropped my foot from the bench, straightening to a stand. "I'm cooking her dinner."

From across the room came a chuckle. Malik and I glanced at Wolf, who'd joined us for the workout.

"What?" I asked, picking up my bag.

"It's a good look on you," he said, following me out.

"What is?"

"Domestic bliss."

I chuckled, giving his arm a little punch. "Thanks, dude."

Outside the gym, a lone photographer hovered, waiting for Wolf to emerge. He snapped some pictures, calling out questions designed to provoke a response.

Wolf's jaw clenched, his head dipping as he glanced away, shielding his face as best he could.

"Jesus, Wolf. Didn't realise it was this bad." Malik looked over at the paparazzi. "You want us to take care of it?"

"Nah, it's not worth the hassle." He ran a hand through his hair. "Same time tomorrow?"

"Yep."

"Sounds good."

I watched Wolf head down the street, frustrated as fuck for my friend that even here, in a place he should feel safe, dirtbags like the guy across the road could find him.

"You know," Malik commented, staring at the photographer. "I always thought being famous would be awesome. Money, fame, women. To be honest, it just seems like a shit-ton of headaches followed by loneliness."

I nodded.

"Alright, bro." Malik lifted a fist, bumping it with me. "See you tomorrow. Say hi to Yazzy for me."

"Will do."

I walked the few streets to Yasmin's apartment, marvelling at the difference a week could make. A week ago, I'd never have even dared wish that Yasmin could be mine, and yet here I was, walking to her apartment for dinner.

And more.

I blew out a huff, my cock thickening in anticipation.

I was trying to be a good guy and slow us the fuck down, but damn. The woman was hotter than sin, tasted better than chocolate, and had me in a perpetual state of arousal.

Dangerous magic.

I sprang up the steps to her apartment, rapping a knuckle on the door.

She pulled it open, holding out a key. "Too soon to give you this?"

I laughed, leaning forward to snatch it from her. "Fuck no."

That issue sorted, I immediately entered, kicking the door shut and advancing on her.

"Caleb!"

I backed her up, dropping my bag on her entry floor, pressing her back into the wall, kissing my way down her neck to her collarbone.

"Mm?" I murmured, grazing teeth against the seam of her neck.

"W-What about dinner?" She asked, her tone half-hearted, her fingers delving into my hair to hold me against her.

"I need some dessert first."

I claimed her mouth with a rough kiss, forcing her to open to me, taking every advantage her acquiescence allowed. I fucked her mouth with mine, brutal and demanding, and she met me kiss for a hungry kiss.

My cock pressed against the zipper of my jeans as my hands floated down her sides, gripping her skirt and hiking it up.

"Caleb!"

"Told you," I said, dropping to my knees. "Dessert first."

I hooked one finger into her underwear, drawing the wet material to the side, the scent of her arousal decorating the air. With a possessive growl, I placed my mouth on her pretty little pussy, her taste exploding on my tongue.

Yasmin bucked, her body bowing as I licked her slit, my tongue dancing along her sensitive flesh. She gripped my hair, her hands fisting the strands.

"More," she groaned, head tipping back. "There, there, there!"

With a grin, I gave in, offering her more, licking and sucking, my free hand snaking around to palm the full globe of her ass.

With a cry, she came, her release coating my face, her sweet body clenching under me.

Fuck yes.

I surged up, hooking my arms around her back and boosting her up. She wrapped her arms and legs around me, holding on.

"Where are you—" Yasmin broke off with a laugh as I began to walk toward her bedroom. "Are we finally doing this?"

"Finally?" I asked with a laugh. "What do you mean, finally?"

She shrugged, peppering kisses over my neck. "Just that I was ready a week ago, and we've done nothing but oral and fingering and licking and—"

I stopped short, staring down at her. "Wait. You *want* me to go fast?"

She pulled back a little, shifting one hand to cup my cheek. "Caleb, not to freak you out, but I'm in love with you. Totally and completely." She searched my face, grinning at whatever she saw. "I don't want to wait. I want our life together to start. Now."

With a groan, I lowered my head to kiss her, all control lost.

With my arms full of my perfect woman, and my lips tasting the sweetness of her, I fumbled my way to her bedroom, tripping on the corner of her rug. With a squealing laugh, she clutched me, both of us landing sideways on the bed.

I rolled, pulling her on top of me, our bodies creating delicious friction. Yasmin nipped at my chin, kissing her way down my neck to suck at my collarbone.

"Babe, come back up here."

"Nope." She sat up, straddling my thighs, her hands going to my shirt. "Take this off."

I lifted, pulling at my shirt and tossing it to one side. With a lusty sigh, her hands came up, roaming over my chest.

"You're so beautiful," she whispered, her gaze focused on her fingers, which were tracing the plains and ridges of my abs.

"Beautiful? Nah, that's you." I lifted the hem of her dress, pulling it up her body, revealing her skin in agonisingly slow detail. "Fucking gorgeous."

Pulling her dress free, I gazed at my gorgeous woman, her wet panties and demi-bra the only scraps of fabric left on her body.

With a growl, I fisted her hair, bringing her

mouth back to mine. Nipping and sucking at her lips, our tongues tangling, I found the clasp of her bra, unclipped it and ripped the flimsy contraption down her arms.

Her breasts bounced free, her nipples taut. I couldn't resist pulling back to cup them, feeling the weight of them in my hands, my thumbs grazing her golden skin before I leaned down, my mouth closing around her areola, her body arching as my tongue teased her little nip.

"Caleb!" Her gasp left me harder than stone. My cock, already rigid, jumped, pulsing with a need to be in her.

Soon.

I played with her nipples, discovering their taste, committing her likes and wants to memory. Yasmin had many erogenous zones, my favourite being the curve of her ass. I'd touched that spot yesterday, and she'd exploded under me, so desperate for me to touch her again that she'd begged me to palm her ass.

Remembering that, I swapped breasts, my mouth making amends to her poorly neglected nipple as my free hand slid down her body, coming to the curve of her generous butt.

With a needy fucking moan, Yasmin rolled off me, falling onto the bed, her body wiggling as she fought to get her soaked panties off.

I couldn't help the primal satisfaction I got from knowing they were wet because of me.

"There," she kicked them away, immediately twisting and reaching for me again. "Now."

My hands slid down her body, one cupping her ass, the other immediately playing with the sensitive skin of her pussy, chuckling darkly when she whimpered, her hips making little thrusts toward me.

"More?" I asked, my fingers still tracing the outline of her slit.

"Fuck yes."

I parted her, immediately finding her clit, circling and rubbing in a way that was guaranteed to drive her crazy.

With a cry, she fell back, her eyes closing, her mouth parted, my name a chanting praise on her lips.

Her hand snaked between us, fisting my cock through my pants.

Fuck!

I pulled back, catching her wrist and gently pulling. Her eyes flew open, her cheeks flushed.

"Did I do it wrong?"

"Never," I assured her, kissing her swollen lips. "But I'm gonna come if you keep that up."

She rose up on one elbow, cocking an eyebrow at me. "So why don't you?"

With a curse, I shoved off the bed, shucking

my pants and briefs, and came back to her. She laughed, welcoming me with open arms.

We kissed, hands stroking, flaming the burning need between us. Her hand began a leisurely glide down my body, finding my cock.

"Need you," she murmured against my lips.

I settled between her thighs, groaning when she guided my cock to her clit, rubbing the crown against her.

"Naughty girl."

She huffed out a laugh, her eyelids at half-mast, a sexy as fuck grin on her lips as she shifted my cock to her hot little entrance. "Come in me."

I pushed into her, both of us gasping. She was tight, hot, and wet as sin. I could feel her muscles stretching to accommodate me as I thrust, her body bowing.

I paused. "Are you—"

"Keep moving!"

A bark of laughter escaped me as I set a rhythm, slow at first, building us both up.

Don't fucking come. Don't fucking come. Don't you dare fucking come.

Nice guys always finished last, and I refused to be anything less than my best for Yasmin. No matter how fucking hard it was not to unload in her.

"Caleb! More!"

I moved, picking up my pace, one hand bracing me, the other sliding down her body, shifting to find her clit.

I thumbed her, once, twice, pressing and circling, moving my thumb in a counter to my thrusts, not giving her a second of time to recover.

With a scream, fingernails raking down my back, her teeth nipping into the skin at my bicep, Yasmin came. Her pussy gripped my cock, milking me until I had no choice but to spill inside her.

I collapsed on top of Yasmin, my body heaving for breath, hers warm beneath me.

"Love you," I told her, panting. "I love you so fucking much, Yasmin. I shouldn't have ever waited this long."

She pushed me a little, moving me off her. "Why did you?"

I sighed, my body cooling, regaining my breath. We settled into each other, snuggling. With absent thought, I ran a hand across her stomach, tracking small hearts on her skin.

"Part of it was that I didn't want to lose you. Having you in my life, even if it was just as a friend, was better than not having any of you at all."

She shook her head. "Meanwhile, I was scared you didn't see me this way."

I dropped a kiss on her shoulder. "Let's just say that we're both fools."

"Agreed."

We sealed it with a kiss, murmuring promises against each other's lips.

"Dinner?" She asked, hearing my stomach rumble.

"Nah, I need more dessert first."

I pulled her onto me, her laughing squeal hardening my dick once more.

"Ride me, Yasmin."

She grinned, gripping my cock and guiding it to her. "As you wish, Mr. Prince."

And with that, all my dreams came true.

EPILOGUE ONE

Yasmin

I lifted my arms, closed my eyes, and took a second to memorise this moment. Material glided down my skin, silk encasing my body.

"Ready?" Farrah asked from behind me.

"Go ahead."

Eyes still closed, I adjusted the bodice of my dress on my chest, holding it while Farrah tightened the strays at my back, pulling the corset tight.

"Okay, you can look."

I opened my eyes, staring at myself in the full-length mirror. Tears prickled, my breath catching in my throat.

"Gorgeous," Farrah breathed beside me

while a photographer hovered, capturing my emotion. "Absolutely stunning."

The wedding dress, my own creation, hugged my curves. The colour, a unique oyster white, set off my skin tone.

This is the dress I'm getting married in.

Laughed bubbled up, joy mixing with anticipation, burning away the tears. I turned from my reflection, laughing at Farrah as she dabbed at the corner of her eyes.

"Really?" I asked, putting my hands on my hips. "You promised."

"I know!" She flapped a hand in my direction. "Only... it's just as you wished. You and Caleb. You're perfect together, and I couldn't be happier for you."

We embraced, holding each other tight.

"Alright." I stepped back, wiping my face. "Make-up good?"

"Yep."

"Hair?"

Farrah scrutinised me as I turned from side to side. "Perfect."

"So, we're ready?"

She grinned, picking up a small bundle of flowers and handing them to me. "Yep, you're ready."

With a huffing laugh, we left the bridal

suite, walking the short distance down the road to the church.

To my husband.

To Caleb.

~

Caleb

Holy fuck.

Yasmin looked like a goddess as she floated down the aisle, Malik escorting her on one arm, her father on the other. At the end of the aisle, she stopped, kissing both of them and leaving them behind to walk the remaining steps to me, making it clear that this was no man giving her away, it was her choosing me.

And thank Christ for that.

Linking my fingers with hers, the world moving at a glacial pace and light speed all at once. I tried to commit each moment to memory, tried to remember how she looked, the words we committed to each other.

Instead, when I looked back, I'd remember her smile, her laughter, and the taste of her kiss.

And this moment.

"...so, raise your glasses," Farrah held up her glass, microphone in one hand, glass in the other. "A toast to the luckiest bastard in the world, and to my best friend – the new mister and missus Yasmin Prince."

Laughing, the room toasted us, glasses clinking, Yasmin leaning over to kiss me. I hooked a hand in her hair, holding her to me for just a beat too long.

"And now," Farrah said from the stage. "The first dance."

Wolf sat on the stage, a guitar cradled on his lap. With a grin, he lifted it, settling it down and adjusting his microphone as I led my beautiful bride to the dance floor.

"Congratulations," Wolf said into the microphone, plucking one chord as Farrah settled beside him, smoothing wrinkles from her long, emerald green silk dress. "I was lucky enough to be there at the start of this beautiful relationship." He grinned. "And maybe had a hand in pushing you two along."

Yasmin leaned into me, laughing. I couldn't resist leaning down to taste her joy.

In his soulful voice, Wolf began singing Ed Sheeran's Perfect.

I gathered Yasmin in my arms, swaying with her as Wolf and Farrah sang.

"Are you happy?" She asked, tilting her face up to smile at me.

"Babe, you shouldn't ever need to ask that

question." I leaned my forehead against hers. "Everything I've ever wished for is in my arms. You're my soul, Yasmin."

With music in our ears and laughter on our lips, we danced through the night, celebrating our love.

EPILOGUE TWO

Caleb

Fifteen years later

I side-shuffled down the row, mumbling apologies and attempting to avoid stepping on people's toes and belongings.

"Hey," Yazzy whispered when I finally dropped into the seat beside her. "You're just in time."

I blew out a breath, leaning across to kiss her on the cheek. "Thanks for saving me a seat."

She grinned, as gorgeous today as she'd ever been. "I had to fend off the dance mum brigade. You're lucky I love you because Ariel Steele has been eyeing off that seat for the last thirty minutes."

I grinned, pressing my thigh into hers. "Was it about to get messy?"

She held up her hands, making claws. "I might have needed you to bail me out later."

"Good thing I'm—"

"Shhhh!"

We both twisted, looking behind us to see one of the dance mums glaring at us.

"Sorry," I said with a wince.

We turned back around, Yasmin's shoulders shaking with barely concealed laughter.

"Hush," I whispered, praying psycho mum behind us wouldn't hear. "We have to be adults."

Her shoulders shook harder, her hand rising to press against her lips as she attempted to stifle her laughter.

"Next up we have our junior class performing a jazz number to Bohemian Rhapsody. Take it away class!"

Out onto the stage, the young dancers pranced, taking up position and holding as the lights dimmed.

"Where is she?" Yasmin whispered.

"Two from the front on the left."

"Got her."

We watched proudly as our youngest daughter began the routine, her smile wide, her joy contagious as she shimmied and shifted her way through the complex moves. With a flourish, the number finished and we surged to our feet—cheering our applause.

Behind us, I heard psycho mum scoff but I didn't care, our girl was amazing.

As they pranced off stage, Yasmin and I resumed our seats, exchanging a grin.

"You know," I whispered, leaning in to press my forehead against hers. "I could go another baby."

"No. We agreed, five is enough."

"But six means even numbers."

"Six means an even bigger minivan."

"We could do it."

She slapped me playfully. "No."

I nuzzled her cheek, grinning when she yielded to me. "Please?"

"No."

"Can we just practice then?"

She twisted slightly, ignoring the shh-ing noises coming from psycho mum. "Mm, I think we could arrange that."

I leaned forward, capturing her lips with mine. "Love you, Yazzy."

"Forever and always."

This book was sugar and spice and all things nice 'cause Yazzy and Caleb are perfect. Honestly, they're

total #CoupleGoals. I hope you loved reading their
too cute for words love story!

If you loved this book, be sure to check out the bonus
slice of life on my website. You can also check out the
next in the Capricorn Cove series.
You Sleigh Me features Farrah and Wolf and some
ASMR goodness!

www.EvieMitchell.com

If you enter the code **EBOOK10** you can get 10% off
your purchase from my website.

Be sure to also sign up for my newsletter or check
out my website for more book news.

ABOUT THE AUTHOR

Evie Mitchell is a thirty-something romance author (she/her/hers) living with disability. She believes in inclusion, accessibility, and fierce romance. Her loves include steamy romance novels, her husband, their THREE sausage dogs (heaven help her), and her ever-growing collection of book-related mugs.

As a woman with a diverse work history including in areas such as emergency response, event management, human rights, disability access, and security - her books are filled with true stories (bridezillas), worst-case scenarios (malfunctioning dresses), and her favourite tropes (one-bed).

Evie specialises in fiercely inclusive happily ever afters.

ALSO BY EVIE MITCHELL

Capricorn Cove Series

The Shake-Up

Double the D

Muffin Top

The Mrs. Clause

New Year Knew You

Double Breasted

As You Wish

You Sleigh Me

Resolution Revolution

Meat Load

Larsson Siblings Series

Thunder Thighs

Clean Sweep

The X-list

Reality Check

The Christmas Contract

Dogg Pack Books

Puppy Love

<u>Bad English</u>

<u>The Frock Up</u>

<u>Pier Pressure</u>

All Access Series

Knot My Type

Love Flushed

Nameless Souls MC Series

<u>Runner</u>

<u>Wrath</u>

<u>Ghost</u>

<u>Shield</u>

Elliot Security Series

<u>Rough Edge</u>

<u>Bleeding Edge</u>